SKER
5-18h

W9-BJT-924

PJ MASKS
Owlette and the Giving Owl

Based on the episode
"Owlette and the Giving Owl"

Ready-to-Read

Simon Spotlight
New York   London   Toronto   Sydney   New Delhi

SIMON SPOTLIGHT
An imprint of Simon & Schuster Children's Publishing Division
1230 Avenue of the Americas, New York, New York 10020
This Simon Spotlight edition September 2017
Adapted by Daphne Pendergrass from the series PJ Masks
For information about special discounts for bulk purchases, please contact
Simon & Schuster Special Sales at 1-866-506-1949 or business@simonandschuster.com.
Manufactured in the United States of America 0817 LAK
10 9 8 7 6 5 4 3 2 1
ISBN 978-1-5344-0376-5 (hc)
ISBN 978-1-5344-0375-8 (pbk)
ISBN 978-1-5344-0377-2 (eBook)

Today is show-and-tell!
Amaya is excited to show the
class her giving owl statue.

"But your aunt told you to give away the statue," Connor says.

"Giving makes you feel good," Greg says. Amaya does not want to give away the statue.

Amaya, Greg, and Connor walk into class. Someone stole all the show-and-tell things!

This looks like a job for the PJ Masks!

Greg becomes Gekko!

Connor becomes

Catboy!

Amaya becomes Owlette!

They are the

PJ Masks!

Catboy hears
moths with his
Super Cat Ears.

The moths lead
them to Luna Girl!

Luna Girl goes to steal more things.

The PJ Masks follow.

Oh no! Luna Girl
steals the
giving owl statue!

The statue is perfect.
"I do not want the
other stuff anymore,"
Luna Girl tells her moths.

"Let her keep the statue,"
Catboy tells Owlette.
"She says she will
return the other stuff."

"No!" Owlette says.

"It is mine!"

She takes the giving owl
from Luna Girl.

Luna Girl is mad.

She steals more stuff!

While the heroes put
the stolen things back,
Luna Girl takes
the giving owl again!
It is all she wants.

"Can she keep the statue?" Gekko asks. "You are supposed to give it away anyway."

Owlette does not want
to give away the
giving owl.

The PJ Masks return
to the Luna Lair.
There is a force field
around it.

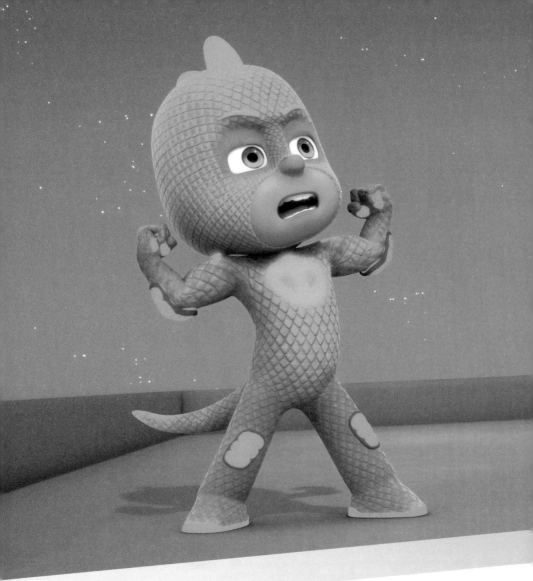

Luna Girl jumps out!

She freezes Gekko

with her Luna Magnet!

Luna Girl freezes

Catboy too!

"Time to be a hero,"
Owlette says.
"You can have the
statue if you let Catboy
and Gekko go."

"No!" Luna Girl says.

She tries to freeze

Owlette next!

Owlette creates wind
with her owl wings. The
wind makes Luna Girl
drop the statue and her
Luna Magnet!

Gekko and Catboy are free!

Owlette takes the giving

owl back.

"I am sorry," Luna Girl says.